Henry F

MW00714832

A Biography

Julie Haydon

A Biography

A biography is a true story. It is about a person's life. Most biographies are about famous people. Some biographies are about people who are not famous.

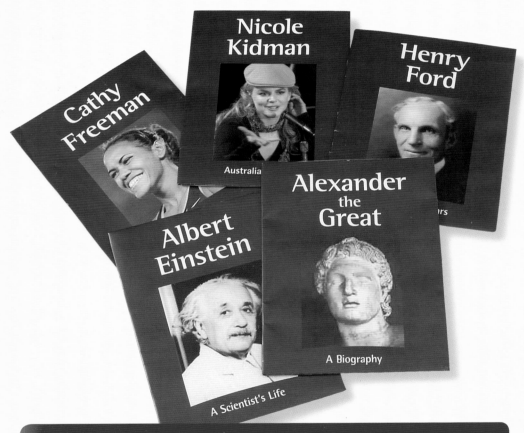

Note: A person can write the story of his or her own life. This story is called an autobiography.

So how do you write a biography?

I've found biographies on:
- actors
- writers
- sports people

And I've found biographies on:
- famous people from the past
- scientists
- people who lived during bad times

The Subject

Choose a person to write about. This person will be the **subject** of your biography.

We have to write a biography. The **theme** is transport.

Let's make a list of all the subjects we can think of.

Note

A person who writes a biography is called a biographer.

Choose a subject that you like. You want to enjoy writing your biography.

Amelia Earhart

Henry Ford

Greg LeMond

Note Sometimes you can find many biographies on the same subject.

People in Transport

Amelia Earhart (pilot)
Henry Ford (Ford cars) ✔
Neil Armstrong (astronaut)
Greg LeMond (cyclist)
Michael Schumacher (racing car driver)
Captain Edward J. Smith (captain of the *Titanic*)

Write a list of questions about your subject. The questions will help you look for important facts about your subject.

Why is Henry Ford famous?
Where and when was he born?
Who was his family?
What was his **childhood** like?

Where did Henry Ford go to school?

What were his **hobbies**?

What work did he do?

When did he die?

Note Remember that people will read your biography. They may not know anything about the subject.

Step 3   The Facts

Find facts about your subject.

You can find facts:

- in books
- on the **Internet**
- in newspapers
- by talking to people.

I went to the library. I found some books on Henry Ford.

Try to talk to your subject if he or she is alive.

Making Notes

Read about your subject and make notes. Write the answers to your questions. Write down important facts only.

Note Keep your notes short.

Why is Henry Ford famous?

He started a car company in 1903. It was called the Ford Motor Company. Most people did not have cars then. The company made lots of good cars. The cars were cheap. Lots of people could buy the cars.

Where and when was he born?

Michigan, United States of America, in 1863.

Who was his family?

His parents were William and Mary Ford.

What was his childhood like?

He grew up on a farm. He did not like farm work. He wanted to learn about machines.

Where and When

Think about where and when your subject lived. What was it like to live in that place? What was it like to live in that time? Make notes about the place and time.

a very old photo of an American farm

Henry Ford was born in America in 1863. Lots of people lived and worked on farms then.

a horse-drawn wagon, from 1886

Most people did not drive cars then. They walked or they rode horses. Horses pulled vehicles too.

Note Look at photographs of your subject. What do they tell you about your subject's life?

Plan your biography. Think about how you want to write it. You are telling the story of a person's life. Make it as exciting as you can.

early American farmers

Let's start our biography with when Henry Ford was born. Then we can write that he was born on a farm, but he did not like farm work.

Note You will know a lot about your subject by now. Only put the important facts in your biography.

Boss of the Road

THE LATEST AND BEST

The FORDMOBILE with **$850**
detachable tonneau

FORD MOTOR COMPA

696 MACK AVENUE

DET

This new light touring car fills the demand for an automobile between a runabout and a heavy touring car is positively the most machine on the ma ing overcome all such as smell, noi common to all of Auto Carriag simple that a b run it.

For beauty of fin equaled — and we **immediate** deli We haven't space enough enter into its mechanical de tail, but if you are interested in the **newest** and most **advance** facture partic

Then we can explain that he liked machines. Later, he started the Ford Motor Company.

Write your biography on a piece of paper. Or you can type it on a computer. When you have finished, read it carefully. Make sure there are no mistakes in it.

The biography is almost finished. Let's check it for mistakes. Then we will print it.

Then we can write a **timeline**.

Note You may want to add a timeline to your biography.

Henry Ford: A Biography

by Isabella and Matthew

Henry Ford was born in 1863. He was born on a farm in Michigan, USA. His parents were William and Mary Ford. Henry went to a small, **local** school.

Henry did not like farm work. He liked machines. He took machines apart to see how they worked. He made machines too.

When Henry was older, he made a car. He made the car in a shed behind his house. Most people did not have cars then. Horses pulled most vehicles.

In 1903, Henry Ford started a car company. It was called the Ford Motor Company. The company made lots of good cars. The cars were cheap. Lots of people could buy them. Soon, millions of people were driving Ford cars.

Henry Ford died when he was 83.

A Ford car. 1919

Henry Ford – A Timeline

1863 Born in Michigan, USA

1879 Moves to a city to work

1896 Finishes making his first car

1903 Starts the Ford Motor Company

1947 Dies at the age of 83

The Steps

Writing a Biography

1 Choose a subject.

2 Write a list of questions about your subject.

3 Find facts about your subject.

4 Make notes about your subject.

5 Find out about when and where your subject lived.

6 Plan your biography.

7 Write your biography.

8 Write a timeline.

Glossary

childhood the time when a person is a child

hobbies things people like to do in their free time

Internet lots of computers that are linked together and share information

local not far away

subject the person a biography is about

theme topic

timeline information set out along a line of dates

website pages of information you can go to when you are connected to the Internet

Index